MINECRAFT
STONESWORD SAGA

NEW PETS ON THE BLOCK

© 2022 Mojang AB. All Rights Reserved. Minecraft, the Minecraft logo and the Mojang Studios logo are trademarks of the Microsoft group of companies.

Published in the United States by Random House Children's Books, a division of Penguin Random House LLC, 1745 Broadway, New York, NY 10019, and in Canada by Penguin Random House Canada Limited, Toronto. Random House and the colophon are registered trademarks of Penguin Random House LLC.

rhcbooks.com
minecraft.net

Library of Congress Cataloging-in-Publication Data is available upon request.
ISBN 978-1-9848-5094-2 (trade)
ISBN 978-1-9848-5095-9 (library binding) — ISBN 978-1-9848-5096-6 (ebook)

Cover design by Diane Choi

Printed in the United States of America

10 9 8 7 6 5 4 3

MINECRAFT
STONESWORD SAGA

NEW PETS ON THE BLOCK

By Nick Eliopulos
Illustrated by Alan Batson and Chris Hill

Random House 🏠 New York

MORGAN

ASH

HARPER

PO

JODI

THEO

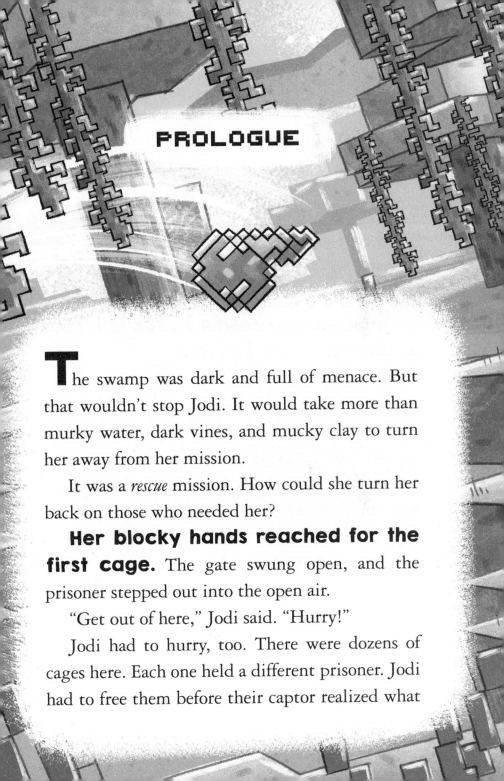

PROLOGUE

The swamp was dark and full of menace. But that wouldn't stop Jodi. It would take more than murky water, dark vines, and mucky clay to turn her away from her mission.

It was a *rescue* mission. How could she turn her back on those who needed her?

Her blocky hands reached for the first cage. The gate swung open, and the prisoner stepped out into the open air.

"Get out of here," Jodi said. "Hurry!"

Jodi had to hurry, too. There were dozens of cages here. Each one held a different prisoner. Jodi had to free them before their captor realized what she was doing. Unless Morgan stopped her first.

"JODI, STOP!" he cried. "We need to talk about this."

But as far as Jodi was concerned, there was nothing to talk about. She opened another cage, and another.

That was as far as she got . . . before they were attacked.

Their unseen enemy struck from the shadows, quick and merciless.

Po was the first to fall.

Theo and Harper were next.

When Morgan was defeated, Jodi was all alone against their attacker.

She knew she had to be brave. She knew everyone was counting on her. She wouldn't back down!

But in the end, it didn't matter. **This was a fight she couldn't win.**

And as Jodi fell to her knees, cursed by some foul magic . . . their enemy laughed.

Jodi wondered if it would be the last sound she ever heard.

Chapter 1

PLEASE HOLD YOUR QUESTIONS UNTIL THE END OF THE PRESENTATION! (BUT YOU CAN OOH AND AHH AS MUCH AS YOU LIKE.)

Jodi Mercado knew how important it was to dress for battle.

When fighting a boss mob, diamond armor was hard to beat.

When dodging fireballs, a shield was quite useful.

When confronting an Enderman, a pumpkin helmet was a smart accessory.

But when it came to a war of words in the real world . . . Jodi chose to wear her very best dress.

"As you can see, animals are adorable," she said. She aimed a red laser pointer at the screen behind her, drawing everyone's attention to the image of a cute, floppy-eared puppy. **She clicked a button on the pointer**—*click!*—and the image changed from the puppy to a kitten with a tiny pink nose. "I would like to hug every animal," she said. "Except for spiders." *Click! Click! Click!* The image changed from kitten to hedgehog to gerbil to gecko.

"Just look at those faces!" Jodi squealed enthusiastically. For a moment, she forgot all about her presentation.

Someone in the audience cleared their throat.

It was a gentle reminder to Jodi that she should stay on topic. She looked down at her notecards, where she had her entire speech written down.

"I love every kind of animal," she read from the final card. "And isn't love the greatest gift of all? Therefore, I think you will agree that I am ready for a pet of my own. Amen. The end. Thank you for listening!"

The small audience broke into eager applause. Jodi grinned from ear to ear as she looked out at them.

Her best friends were all there, gathered in a

meeting room in Excalibur County Public Library. **(They called it Stonesword Library, which was less of a mouthful.)**

Harper Houston cheered from her seat. A whiz with math and science, Harper had helped Jodi with the technological parts of her presentation. She had even created Jodi's one-of-a-kind laser pointer. **It looked like something right out of Minecraft!**

Po Chen whooped and hollered. He could be a goofball, but he was always supportive of his friends. During Jodi's presentation, he had laughed the loudest at her jokes.

Theo Grayson clapped politely. Theo was good with computers, but Jodi wasn't sure he liked animals very much. Even so, he had helped Jodi download all the pictures for her slideshow.

Ash Kapoor waved her hands in silent applause. Although Ash lived in a different city and couldn't be there in person, she had used video software to watch the presentation through Theo's laptop. Her smile lit up the screen.

Even the class hamster, Baron Sweetcheeks,

had his eyes on Jodi. He couldn't cheer for her, but Jodi felt that he was providing excellent emotional support.

Morgan Mercado was another story. Although he clapped, too, he seemed uncertain. Hesitant. Jodi knew her big brother well, and she could tell he was less excited than everybody else.

What was that about? After all, any pet Jodi brought into their home was a pet Morgan could hug, too.

He was probably thinking about Minecraft, Jodi decided. He usually was!

"So?" said Jodi. "What did everybody think? Is this enough to convince my parents that **I'm ready to take care of a pet?"**

"Absolutely," Ash said from the laptop's speakers. "You made a very smart argument."

Harper added, "The part about using eco-friendly poop bags was a nice touch."

"Gross, Harper!" said Po, wrinkling his nose. "Don't say *poop* and *touch* in the same sentence." He and Harper both laughed.

Theo raised his hand. "I wonder if you should say *vertebrates* instead of *animals,*" he suggested. "All the images you used were of animals with a backbone. And I assume you don't want a pet cricket or earthworm." Harper elbowed him. "Oh, but other than that—good job," he added quickly.

Jodi could feel her heart swell with cheerfulness . . . **and hope.** She had wanted a pet for years, and her parents had never agreed to it. They always said no. They said it wasn't the right time for a pet. They told her to wait until she was older.

Well, Jodi had made up her mind: now, at last, was the right time. She was old enough. She was responsible enough! And when her parents heard her presentation after dinner tonight, she was sure they would agree with her.

She was pretty sure, at least.

But when she snuck a glance at Morgan, she saw that he was frowning. **And a dark cloud of worry passed over Jodi's heart.**

Chapter 2

ANIMALS OF THE OVERWORLD! I'LL NEVER GET OVER HOW CUTE THEY ARE.

The next day, Morgan, Jodi, and their friends returned to the library. This time, they weren't there for a meeting room. Instead, they collected a set of special VR headsets from the front desk. The goggles felt electric in Morgan's hands. He gripped his set tightly as he led Jodi, Po, Harper, and Theo to a row of networked computers in the back.

The computers would allow them to play Minecraft together.

And the VR goggles would allow them to live Minecraft together.

Morgan had given up on ever understanding

how the goggles were able to transport them into **the world of their favorite game.** Their science teacher, Doc Culpepper, had done . . . *something* to the goggles, supercharging them somehow. Her experiments were known mostly for going wrong in spectacular ways, but in this case, she had gotten something very right. In the end, he didn't really care *how* they worked. So long as they worked.

He took a seat, booted up the game, and slipped the goggles over his eyes.

The next thing Morgan knew, he was standing in a simple rectangular house. It was just big enough for five beds, a crafting table, a furnace, and a chest of supplies. **There was a single iron door, operated by a button, and there were two torches set into one of the house's stone walls.**

This build didn't have any of the comforts of home. But that was because they wouldn't be staying here for long. They were constantly exploring, going deeper into Minecraft. And right now, they had a mission.

"All right, let's get started," said Morgan. He clicked the button on the wall. The door swung open, and he stepped outside. It was a clear, sunny day in the Overworld. Morgan smiled . . . and then he looked up, and he frowned. **The Fault was plainly visible high above him.** It looked like someone had taken the bright blue sky and just . . . *ripped* it.

"We really need to figure out what that Fault is," said Harper as she stepped outside the house. **"I'M SURE IT'S GETTING BIGGER."**

Theo was giving the rip a long look. He turned and nodded to Harper in agreement with her assessment. "It *is* getting bigger."

"One problem at a time," said Morgan. "First we need to find the next piece of—"

Suddenly, Jodi came bursting out of the house, running at top speed and shouting at the top of her lungs. "Look at that bunny!" she yelled.

"I WANT TO PET THE BUNNY!"

The bunny, it seemed, did not want to be petted. It bounded away, disappearing over a hill.

Jodi didn't follow. She was immediately distracted by a cow. Then a sheep. Then a pig. She ran back and forth across the plain, petting them all. She was definitely not "on mission" at the moment.

"Maybe I'll get a piglet in real life," she said.

Po laughed. His avatar was especially detailed today. Even though he was as blocky as the rest of them, the carefully placed pixels of his outfit made him look almost *fluffy*. Morgan thought he must be a cloud. Or a sheep? She wasn't sure. Po never stuck with one look for long. **He had a huge collection of skins, and he was constantly changing them.**

"Or maybe I should get a pet chicken!" said Jodi. She patted a hen, which flapped and clucked at the attention.

"I guess the presentation went well," Po said.

Jodi flashed a grin. Even in avatar form, it was easy to see how happy she was. "It went so well!" she cried.

"So your parents said yes?" asked Theo.

"They said 'we'll see,'" answered Jodi as she ran circles around a nearby horse. "Which is basically the same thing as yes."

Morgan kept his expression neutral,

and he tried to keep his voice neutral, too. "I don't think you should get your hopes up yet," he told his sister.

"TOO LATE!" She cackled, then started poking around at the edge of a lake. Morgan thought she was probably hoping for a glimpse of an axolotl— even though she should know by now that those mobs are only found way underground. Morgan rolled his eyes.

"Morgan!" Po whispered. "What gives? **YOU'RE BEING SO NEGATIVE."**

"Po's right," Harper said gently. "You could be a little more supportive."

Before answering, Morgan made sure his sister wasn't listening. "You don't understand," he said. "You didn't see my parents' faces during that presentation. They did *not* think getting a pet was a good idea." He shook his head. "Besides, when has 'we'll see' *ever* meant 'yes'?"

"He's got a point," said Theo. **"IN MY EXPERIENCE, PARENTS SAY 'WE'LL SEE' WHEN THEY REALLY MEAN 'NOT IN A MILLION YEARS.' "**

"Exactly," Morgan said.

"But she's so happy," said Po. **"ISN'T THERE SOMETHING YOU CAN DO?"**

"Me?" said Morgan.

"Maybe you could change your parents' minds," said Harper. "If she can't convince them . . . maybe *you* could convince them that she's ready for a pet."

"MAYBE . . . ," said Morgan.

Theo rubbed his blocky chin and gave Morgan a long look. "Morgan . . . you *do* think she's ready for a pet, don't you?"

Morgan hesitated. He wasn't sure how to answer that question.

"You guys!" said Jodi, and Morgan was happy for the interruption. "Does anybody have a bone?

THERE'S A WOLF BY THE TREES, AND I WANT TO GIVE HIM A TREAT."

"What a coincidence," said Po. He did a little twirl. "My avatar skin is a wolf today."

Theo frowned. "Are you sure? I thought you were a sheep."

"Aha! That's what I was going for," said Po. "See, I'm actually a wolf in sheep's clothing."

"SO YOU'RE PO . . . DRESSED AS A WOLF . . . DRESSED AS A SHEEP," SAID THEO.

Po laughed. "Baaah-sically, yeah."

"Let me check my inventory for a bone," Harper said. "I'm pretty sure I have one."

Morgan looked over Jodi's shoulder, and he saw the wolf in the distance. It was standing at the edge of a nearby forest. His sister obviously hoped to tame the wolf by giving it a bone.

"Are you sure you want to do this?" Morgan asked her. "Even digital wolves are a lot of responsibility. **YOU'LL HAVE TO FEED IT AND KEEP IT AWAY FROM LAVA.**"

Jodi waved around the bone that Harper had given her. "Sure I'm sure," she said. "Keeping away from lava is one of my favorite things!"

Morgan and the others followed as Jodi ran up to the wolf. She offered the bone to the animal, and the wolf took it, but no little red hearts appeared around its head. That meant it hadn't been tamed.

"SOMETIMES ONE BONE ISN'T ENOUGH," said Theo. "But you could try again."

Harper shook her head. "I don't have any more bones," she said. "Sorry, Jodi."

"Aw. It's okay," said Jodi. "Lobo Joe here just

wants to be free!"

Lobo Joe that was the wolf's name now, Morgan figured turned to go. It walked across the plain and disappeared from view.

It disappeared from view *very suddenly,* in fact.

"Where did it go?" asked Harper, startled.

"LOBO JOE?" said Jodi. "What happened to you?"

The kids all ran in the direction the wolf had gone.

They didn't see the pit until it was almost too late.

Morgan called, "Stop!" And he threw his arms out to the side. The others skidded to a stop just behind him, at the edge of a large hole.

The hole was full of animals. Not just Lobo Joe, but ocelots and chickens and more. **Several of the animals looked at the wolf with worry in their eyes. But maybe because of the strange situation they found themselves in, the animals mobs were staying calm . . . at least for the moment.**

"They fell into a hole, the poor things," Jodi said. "We should help them."

"We can dig some steps out of the dirt," offered Harper. "Then they can climb back up."

"This reminds me of that time we trapped a bunch of angry bunnies in a pit," Po said, pulling a pickaxe from his inventory. "Good times!"

Morgan nodded slowly. Po was right—perhaps more so than he realized.

The pit had a purpose.

Someone had *dug* this hole in the Minecraft dirt. Someone had trapped these animals on purpose!

Chapter 3

OUT OF THE PIT. INTO THE SWAMP! (I'LL TAKE ANY OTHER OPTION YOU'VE GOT, PLEASE.)

Jodi didn't get mad very often. But when Morgan told her what he suspected, she was furious.

"You think someone set this trap on purpose?" she said. She sputtered and shook. **"BUT . . . BUT WHY WOULD ANYONE WANT TO CAPTURE ALL THESE POOR ANIMALS?"**

A newly freed chicken clucked as it hurried past. To Jodi, the clucking sounded a little like "thank you."

"I don't know who would do this, or why," said Morgan. "I just know that hole didn't look natural. There were loose blocks of dirt around the edges."

"Maybe a creeper exploded," Theo suggested. "There *could* be a simple explanation."

"Maybe," said Morgan. But he didn't seem convinced. His gut was clearly telling him that something strange was happening here.

And then they saw the butterfly.

Butterflies were not a natural occurrence in the world of Minecraft. But when Jodi and her friends accessed the game with their headsets, the version of Minecraft they experienced was sometimes . . . a little different, or even downright bizarre.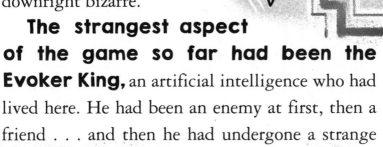

The strangest aspect of the game so far had been the Evoker King, an artificial intelligence who had lived here. He had been an enemy at first, then a friend . . . and then he had undergone a strange transformation. **The Evoker King had split into six different mobs,** each containing a piece of his programming and personality.

And when those mobs were nearby, the kids often saw digital butterflies—mobs that were definitely not a feature in the Vanilla game.

"Did you see that?" said Morgan. "A butterfly just flew by! We need to follow it."

"What? No!" said Jodi. "We have to find out who trapped these animals."

"Jodi," Morgan said, using his most serious "big brother" voice. "That butterfly could lead us to the next piece of the Evoker King. **THAT'S OUR MISSION, REMEMBER?"**

"It's more than just a mission," said Harper. "The Evoker King is our friend, and it's up to us to put him back together again."

"I WANT TO HELP HIM," said Jodi. "You know I do! But I want to help these animals, too."

"Maybe we can do both somehow," Po suggested.

"We can't do two things at once," Morgan said, huffing. "Jodi, you just gave us all a big speech about how responsible you are. Don't you see how irresponsible it is to get distracted from our quest?"

Jodi suddenly wished that Minecraft avatars had laser vision. **She knew one big brother who deserved a face full of laser right now.** She settled for scowling at him.

"Uh, guys?" said Theo. "I do not want to be in the middle of this. Not even a little bit. But—"

"—the butterfly is almost out of sight." Harper finished. "Are we going after it or not?"

Jodi sighed. "Fine. But somebody mark this spot on our map. **WE'RE NOT DONE WITH THIS ANIMAL MYSTERY."**

She tried to keep the frustration out of her voice. But she didn't try very hard.

Morgan almost lost sight of the butterfly more than once. It fluttered between the trees of the forest. The sun was high in the sky, so the leaves cast dark shadows. But with all five of them on the lookout, they were able to stay on the insect's trail.

Morgan hoped that following the butterfly was the right decision. He knew his sister was worried about the animals they had found. He admired her kindness and compassion. But he wanted to put the Evoker King back together more than anything.

Following the butterfly led them out of the forest and into a biome of dark, shallow water.

"IT'S A SWAMP," said Po. He made a face as he pulled his foot out of a puddle.

"It's kind of creepy," said Jodi, and Morgan agreed. Dark vines hung from oak trees, and the water was a murky green instead of blue.

"It's just like any other biome," said Theo. "It's programmed to look gloomy, that's all."

"And there are some unique resources here,"

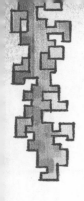

Harper added. "See the lily pads on the water? You can only find them in swamps."

Po turned up his wolfish nose. "I am *not* going into that water," he said.

Theo plucked a light blue flower, and he handed it to Harper. **"BLUE ORCHIDS ARE UNIQUE TO SWAMPS, TOO,"** he said. Harper accepted the flower with a shy smile.

Po also made a face at that.

"Hey, look!" Jodi said. "Somebody built a house out here."

Morgan saw it. It was a boxy wooden structure, and it was built right above the water. Four wooden pillars like stilts kept the house above the muck.

"It's not a house," he whispered. **"IT'S A SWAMP HUT."**

"Okay, sure," Po whispered back. "But why are we whispering?"

"Because swamp huts have another name," Morgan answered. "They're also called *witch huts.*"

As soon as he said those words, **Morgan saw a shape moving behind the hut's windows.** "And there's someone inside," he said.

"What's the big deal?" said Po. "We can handle a witch, right?"

"An ordinary witch? Sure," agreed Morgan. "But look."

Morgan pointed to the roof of the hut. **The butterfly had landed right on top of it.**

Harper gasped. "Do you think the mob in that hut is one of the Evoker Spawn we're looking for?" she asked.

Morgan nodded. "Probably. And if it's anything

like the last two, it will be a lot more dangerous than your average mob. **WE'LL NEED TO BE QUIET . . . AND CAREFUL, AND . . .** Wait." He looked around. "Where's Jodi?"

"UH-OH," said Po, and he pointed.

Jodi was running at top speed, splashing through the shallow water. She wasn't trying to hide. She wasn't trying to be quiet.

And she was heading right for the witch's hut.

Chapter 4

WELCOME TO THE ZOO!
COME FOR THE PANDAS.
STAY FOREVER. . . .

Jodi knew she was taking a big risk. **The creepy house on stilts was obviously not the kind of place she wanted to be.** But as she splashed through the shallow water, she wasn't thinking about the hut. She was thinking about what she had seen *behind* the hut.

"JODI!" her brother hissed. He was quickly catching up to her, and the others were close behind him. "What are you doing?"

"I'm helping," she said. "I'm helping *them.*"

Jodi stepped onto dry land, just a short distance from the swamp hut. There were fences there. *Cages.* They were built from the same spruce and oak as the hut. **And they held just about every animal Jodi had ever seen in Minecraft.**

"Whoa," said Po. "Check out all the animals." He peered between the bars of the nearest cage. "Is that a panda? I forgot Minecraft even *had* pandas."

"THEY ONLY SPAWN IN JUNGLES," Morgan said. He leaned in closer. "It sort of looks like a jungle biome inside the cage, doesn't it? There's bamboo growing in there." He frowned. "That shouldn't happen in a swamp."

"And there," said Harper, pointing at another cage. "The turtle's cage is full of sand and water. It looks like a small beach."

"Someone is recreating the home biome of each animal," Theo said. "There's even an aquarium over there. **IT'S FULL OF DIFFERENT KINDS OF FISH."**

"That panda is just a baby," Jodi said. "It looks so sad!"

"That's just your imagination," said Theo. "It can't be sad. It isn't a real panda."

Before Jodi could disagree, the panda sneezed.

A glob of slime landed nearby.

"Okay, that was somehow both adorable and disgusting at the same time," said Po.

Harper grinned, and she picked up the slimeball. "You never know," she said. "This might come in handy."

"Harper!" said Po, **looking grossed out**— as much as an avatar in a wolf-sheep skin could. "I hope you know how to craft a sink, because you need to wash your hands. Like, right away!"

"A little slime never hurt anybody," said Harper, and she waved her blocky hands in Po's face.

While Po squealed and laughed, Morgan appeared lost in thought. After a long moment, he said, "It's a zoo. But who would make this, and why?"

"IT'S NOT A ZOO," said Jodi. "It's a prison! And whoever built it is obviously the same person who was trapping animals in a pit." She hopped in anger. "It isn't right. It isn't fair. And I'm going to set them all free."

"Now, hold on a minute," said Morgan.

But Jodi didn't listen. She flung open a gate. A goat stepped out, leaving the gravelly, mountainous landscape of its cage. **"BE FREE!"** said Jodi. "Get out of here. Hurry!" The goat bleated once, then hurried past them into the swamp.

Jodi didn't stop there. She ran down the line of cages, throwing open one door after another.

"**JODI, STOP!**" said Morgan. "We need to talk about this."

Just then, an eerie giggle rang out. Jodi froze, confused. The sound was coming from the cage that she had just opened. Inside it, a colorful bird sat atop a log.

"Dude," said Po. "**DID THAT PARROT JUST LAUGH AT US?**"

Jodi saw the worry on her brother's face. "What is it?" she asked. "What's wrong?"

"Well . . . parrots make different sounds depending on what other mobs are nearby," Morgan explained. "They hiss when a creeper is close. They groan when a zombie's around. And that giggle . . . it sounded like . . ."

"Like what?" asked Jodi.

Morgan answered: "**LIKE A WITCH.**"

Jodi turned to look at the nearby hut. A menacing figure loomed in its open doorway. It wore a pointed hat and a dark cloak. And it was watching them with bright green eyes.

It was a witch. It laughed—a wicked, haunting cackle that sent a chill through Jodi's avatar.

And then it attacked.

Po was the first one to be hit. He didn't even have time to draw his sword. A potion struck him square in the back. He flashed red and fell to his knees.

Just one hit, and he was out of the fight.

"WE'RE UNDER ATTACK!" cried Harper, and she fired an arrow. It struck the wood hut with a *thunk.*

"Where did the witch go?" said Theo, and he gripped his sword. "It was right there a second ago."

"Behind you!" yelled Morgan. But his warning came too late. The witch leapt from the shadows, hurling potions at Theo and Harper. As they fell to their knees, **the witch disappeared again, fading into the gloomy darkness of the swamp.**

"THE WITCH IS TOO FAST," said Morgan. "It shouldn't be able to *move* like that—or that fast. That's no normal mob."

Jodi pressed her back against his. "Just keep your eyes open, big brother," she said. **"THE WITCH CAN'T SNEAK UP ON BOTH OF US."**

Morgan and Jodi turned in a slow circle, back to back. They gazed out into the swamp and down the aisles of the strange, swampy zoo.

But when Jodi heard the witch's cackle, it wasn't coming from either of those directions. The sound was coming from *above* them.

Jodi looked up in time to see the witch peering down from atop the nearest cage. The mob hurled a flask at them. It shattered against Morgan, **splashing him with its foul liquid.**

And now Jodi stood alone. She held her sword in one hand and her shield in the other. "I'm not afraid of you," said Jodi. "I'm going to save these animals you've captured. You can't stop me."

"Stop you, hrm," said the witch. The voice was strange and shrill. The mob took a step back, fading into the darkness.

Jodi turned to her brother. **"ARE YOU OKAY?"** she asked him.

And then the witch's shrill voice sounded just behind her. "Stop you, hah!" said the mob.

Jodi felt a splash potion shatter against her back. It didn't hurt . . . but it had a strange and immediate effect on her. Jodi felt suddenly weak— weak, and so, so tired. She dropped to her knees. She couldn't even summon the strength to stand.

"What . . . what is this?" she asked.

"SOME KIND OF SICKNESS," Morgan said

beside her.

Standing above them, the witch cackled in triumph. "Cursed, you are," said the mob. Its speech was odd, full of pauses and purring sounds. "Fix you, hah, I can."

"Do it, then," said Harper. "Lift this . . . this spell or curse or whatever it is you've done to us."

"A PRICE, HRM, YOU MUST PAY," said the witch. It leaned in closer. This mob moved her arm as she talked. That definitely wasn't like any normal Minecraft witch. "A mooshroom of brown. You bring one, hah, to me."

"You want us to bring you . . . a brown cow?"

asked Po. "That's your price?"

"We won't do it," said Jodi. "We won't help you hunt any more animals!"

"Help me, hah, you will," said the witch. "For the cure you seek, hrm, is the *stew* that, hah, **THE MOOSHROOM MAKES.**"

Silence fell over the group. Jodi wanted to argue—she wanted to *fight.* But she could barely crawl.

"QUEST FOR ME, YOU WILL," said the witch. "Over land, hah, and sea, hrm." She opened the gate of a nearby cage. Inside it was a row of neat beds. "But first . . . heh. You rest." She cackled, then added, "Hah-hah-hrm. Rest well . . . **MY PETS.**"

Chapter 5

SUSPICIOUS STEW: IS THE CURE WORSE THAN THE DISEASE?

Theo felt a chill as he removed his VR goggles. Was it the library's air-conditioning? Or . . . could it be the curse of the witch?

He shook his head. **Surely the witch's magic couldn't affect them here, in the real world.** Even so, Theo was thoroughly creeped out. The witch was an adversary unlike any they had faced before.

Although . . . that was only half true. **The witch was faster, more menacing, and much more talkative than a typical Minecraft witch.** There was only one explanation for that. Just like the monstrous Enderman and the mind-controlling cave spider before her, this unique mob *must* be one of the Evoker King fragments. And that meant, even if they *could* fight it . . . they probably shouldn't. They would need a unique approach to the problem.

"I think we have to do what the witch says," Theo said to his friends. **"We need to find a mooshroom and bring it back to her."**

Po sighed. "That sounds like a lot of work. But we definitely need the cure."

"It's not just about the cure, though," said Theo. "If that witch is one of the Evoker Spawn, then we need to show her that we aren't her enemies."

Jodi gripped her goggles tightly. "There has to be another way. We can't do her dirty work for her. Not if it means capturing another poor animal. **Who knows what's she's up to?!"**

"We don't have a lot of choices," said Morgan. "We're her prisoners . . . because *somebody* ran into danger without a plan."

Jodi scowled at him. "*You're* the one who runs off every time a butterfly floats by!"

"Blaming each other won't help us right now," said Harper. **"Instead of pointing fingers, we should focus on what we can do next."**

Po scratched the top of his head. "Maybe we can figure out the cure by ourselves," he suggested. "What did the witch say about soup?"

"Stew," Theo corrected him.

"And not just any stew," said Morgan. **"Suspicious stew.** Believe it or not, you can get it from mooshrooms."

"That does not sound delicious," said Po. "But does it mean we could cure ourselves? Could we get this . . . suspicious stew . . . and not give her the mooshroom?"

"Or could we make the stew ourselves?" suggested Harper. **"I'm certain it can be crafted."**

"We don't have enough information," Morgan said, shaking his head. "Suspicious stew is unpredictable. It can have all sorts of different effects on a player. And when you get it from a mooshroom, the stew's exact effects depend on what the mooshroom has eaten." He shrugged. "So the witch only told us *part* of the cure. **We know it's suspicious stew, but we don't know what kind."**

"We're really trapped, then," said Harper. "We have to do what the witch says."

"Easier said than done," Theo said. "Brown mooshrooms are **extremely rare**. They're even rarer than the red variety."

"What about breeding one?" Morgan suggested. "If you pair two red mooshrooms together and they have a baby, there's a chance the baby will be brown."

"Yeah," Theo said, scoffing. "A one-in-1,024 chance, to be specific."

"Never tell me the odds!" Po replied, having no idea exactly how good or bad those odds were.

Theo dragged his feet as they all walked up to the front of the library and turned in their headsets. He was a programmer, so he couldn't help but think of the odds. And the odds really were not in their favor this time.

As they left the library and stepped out into the

sunshine, Jodi said, "I still don't like it. **I wish we knew why she wants a mooshroom.** Does she really just want to keep it in a cage?"

"Does it matter?" Theo said. "It's not a real animal."

"But they *seem* real," said Jodi. "They eat food, and they have babies, and they run away from you if you hurt them."

"They do those things because they're programmed to do them," said Theo. **"They're just little bits of code.** They don't have feelings."

"Well, you could say the same thing about the Evoker King," said Po. "But we care about him, right?"

"Sounds like a very serious discussion," said a voice. **Theo turned to see Mr. Malory, the library's media specialist, sitting beneath the library's famous sculpture of a sword.** He was on a break, and enjoying a snack.

"What do you think, Mr. Malory?" asked Theo. "Do NPCs and virtual animals have feelings?"

Mr. Malory thought about it for a moment.

"They don't have feelings, no. Not as we understand them."

"See?" Theo said to Jodi.

"However!" said the librarian, holding up a finger. "That doesn't mean we should treat them as if they don't matter. **It's a fine idea to show compassion to all creatures, whether they can appreciate it or not.**"

"Even if that slows down your progress in a game?" Po asked. **"Or makes it harder to win?"**

"That's what I was thinking," said Morgan. "Isn't it sort of a waste of time to be nice to creatures that aren't even real?"

"I don't think compassion is ever a waste of time," Mr. Malory answered. "Positivity, kindness, patience . . . these are all crucial skills to develop. Not just because of what they do for the people or animals around you. You benefit, too. **Put positivity out into the world, and good things happen.**"

"I agree with Mr. Malory," said Jodi. And then she stuck her tongue out at Theo, which did *not*

feel especially compassionate.

Theo sighed. He didn't have the energy for a larger argument. But in his heart, he was worried.

Jodi's compassion had already gotten them into a very difficult situation. If she cared more about digital mushroom-covered cows than about being cured . . . **would the witch's curse ever be broken?**

Chapter 6

AN ITSY-BITSY SPIDER CAUSED A GREAT BIG PROBLEM!

It was several days later when Harper and her friends finally had time to put on the VR goggles and enter Minecraft again.

They had expected to appear in the cage where the witch had left them. **Instead, their beds and their spawn point had been moved to the edge of the swamp.** A nearby chest contained a single item: a map, marked with the location of an island.

The kids knew immediately that the island must be the nearest mushroom field—the only biome where mooshrooms could spawn. Clearly, the witch was eager for their quest to begin.

All things considered . . . it didn't get off to a great start.

They had only been walking a short while before they were attacked. **It was a spider, lunging at them from the shadows.** At first, Harper wasn't worried. They had fought—and defeated—more spiders than they could count.

"I've got it," Morgan said, and he swung his sword in a wide arc.

The spider leapt, easily avoiding his attack. Then it sprang at Po, biting him.

"OW!" cried Po. "What did I do?"

Harper saw her opening, and she took it. Running forward, she attacked the spider while it was still facing Po.

Her sword attack hurt the spider. She could tell by the way it flashed red.

But it didn't hurt the spider as much as it should have.

"We are in so much trouble," she said as the spider turned its angry red eyes in her direction.

It was just a normal, everyday spider. It should have been an easy battle for any one of them.

But the witch's curse had changed everything.

The spider lunged for Harper. She stepped back, striking it again with her sword. At that same instant, Theo shot it with an arrow. Finally, it fell, disappearing in a pixelated puff of dust.

"Whew. That was *much* tougher than it should have been," said Harper, verbalizing her earlier observation.

"IT'S LIKE WE'RE NOOBS ALL OVER AGAIN," said Po. He bit into an apple so that he could regain his lost health.

"It's worse than that," Theo said. "This 'curse' . . . I think it's a **DEBUFF**."

"A what, now?" asked Jodi.

"A debuff," Theo repeated. **"IN A VIDEO GAME, AN ADVANTAGE IS CALLED A BUFF.** Like . . . when a potion makes you stronger, or a blessing makes you faster. That's a buff."

"So a debuff is the opposite," Harper said.

"Correct," Theo continued. **"IT'S A DISADVANTAGE.** Something that makes you less powerful."

"There are plenty of buffs and debuffs in Minecraft," Morgan added. "Like Weakness, which makes your attacks less powerful."

"I CERTAINLY FELT WEAK AGAINST THAT SPIDER," said Harper, and she picked up the string and eyeball left behind by the defeated mob. "We had to hit it a lot more times than we usually would."

"That's why I'm wearing my special 'chicken pox' skin," said Po. "In real life, I feel fine. But here, I feel totally under the weather. And my pox shows it."

Everyone looked at Po, **whose avatar today was a chicken covered in polka dots**. "Oh, *now* I get it," said Morgan.

"You know chickens don't actually get chicken pox, right?" said Theo. "That virus only affects humans. And apes, I think."

Po flapped his feathered arms. "Well, a spotted gorilla would just look ridiculous," he said. "Ba-kaw!"

"I like this look on you," said Harper, and she patted his head.

"Careful," Po clucked. **"I MIGHT BE CONTAGIOUS."**

Theo sighed. *"Anyway,"* he said, eager to get back on topic. "I don't think there's anything magical—or even that mysterious—about this so-called witch's curse. It's a debuff—a way of messing with the code."

"Then we'd better be careful," said Morgan, and he held up the map for all to see. "Because we've got a long way to go. **AND I'M SURE THAT SPIDER ISN'T THE LAST HOSTILE MOB WE'LL HAVE TO FIGHT.**"

Morgan's words proved true. Over the days-long voyage, the group encountered an endless series of dangers. They stayed out of the shadows and tried to avoid fighting whenever they could. When a fight was unavoidable, they tried to attack from a distance. **It took a lot of arrows to defeat a zombie,** but it felt safer than getting close enough to swing a sword.

They went over or around mountains instead of cutting through them. When they spotted an Enderman in the distance, **they quickly looked away.** When they saw an illager tower, they crossed a lake to avoid it.

At first, they stopped only to gather apples and other food items. Keeping their health up was more important than ever, and that meant keeping their bellies full. But on the third night of their voyage, phantoms appeared in the night sky. **Morgan panicked.** He knew how deadly the flying mobs could be, so he had insisted that the group stop and rest rather than pushing ahead through a night full of dangers. Despite their hurry, nobody had disagreed with him.

When they finally saw the mushroom island in the distance, they let out a cheer. But it was a small, weak cheer. They didn't have much energy to spare, and it was too soon to celebrate.

"We could swim," said Morgan. **"BUT CROSSING ON BOATS WILL BE SAFER."**

Theo started digging up the grass at the water's edge. "While you all build boats, I'll grow some wheat. We'll need it, so that the mooshroom will follow us."

"Follow us to its *doom*," said Jodi glumly.

Jodi couldn't stay too gloomy for long. Under the light of the full moon, the mushroom fields biome was strange and wonderful, with a ground made of some spongy purple material—her brother called it *mycelium*—**and towering toadstools the size of trees.** But by far the most amazing part of the biome was the mooshrooms themselves. The peaceful mobs roamed around the small island, munching on grass and giving the kids curious looks.

"There are a lot of mooshrooms here," said Po. "But they're all red."

"I had an idea about that," said Morgan. **"RED MOOSHROOMS CHANGE TO BROWN WHEN THEY'RE STRUCK BY LIGHTNING.** So if we can lead one into a storm . . ."

Po looked up at the sky. Other than the Fault, it was totally clear. "I'd ask what the odds are of that plan working," he said, "but I'm afraid Theo would actually tell me the answer."

"I don't know *everything,*" said Theo. "Although I could run some calculations. . . ."

Morgan sighed. "I'll admit: it's a long shot. BUT IT'S EITHER THAT OR WE ROAM THE OVERWORLD LOOKING FOR ANOTHER MUSHROOM BIOME. THAT COULD TAKE MONTHS."

"And in our current condition, it's dangerous to go roaming around," added Theo. "I think Morgan's idea is the best we've got. Let's grab a red mooshroom and get out of here."

Harper turned to Jodi. "You could choose which mooshroom will go with us," Harper suggested.

"You're good with animals, after all."

Jodi nodded solemnly. "Let me talk to them," she said. "I'll figure out which one is bravest."

As Jodi went from one mooshroom to the next, whispering into their ears and patting their backs, Theo turned to Harper. "She knows they're all identical, right? **I MEAN, THE CODE IS EXACTLY THE SAME FOR EVERY RED MOOSHROOM.**"

Harper shrugged. "Maybe Jodi sees something we don't."

"I've got a question," said Po. "How do you get a mooshroom onto a boat?" He paused for a moment. "That sounds like the setup to a joke, but I'm really asking."

"I've got that figured out," answered Harper. She pulled the slimeball from her inventory. "I'm awfully glad I held on to this."

"Gross," said Po, but he laughed as he said it.

Chapter 7

INTRODUCING: MICHAEL G! NOT TO BE CONFUSED WITH MICHAEL C OR MICHAEL P.

Jodi had made her selection. She didn't feel *good* about it. **But she'd chosen the poor mooshroom they would take away from this island paradise and hand over to an obviously up-to-no-good witch.**

Now she only had to make introductions.

"Morgan. Po. Harper and Theo," she said, drawing their attention. "I'd like you to meet the newest member of our team. This is Michael G."

Michael G mooed, as if saying hello. Or maybe he was asking what in the world was happening.

"Hello, uh, Michael," said Morgan.

"Welcome to the team!" said Po, and then he whispered, "I'm not *really* a chicken."

"Michael G," said Harper. **"THAT'S AN INTERESTING NAME."**

"It doesn't seem very fitting," said Theo. "Are there a lot of other Michaels here?"

Jodi crossed her arms. "It's a pun, smart guy. Don't you get it?"

Harper laughed, obviously the first one to get the joke. Everyone else looked at her expectantly. "The scientific study of mushrooms is called mycology," she explained. "Say it fast, and it sort of sounds like, well . . ." She turned to the mooshroom. **"IT'S NICE TO MEET YOU, MICHAEL G. DO YOU MIND IF WE PUT THIS ON YOU?"**

Harper held up a short rope, tied like a lasso. "Where'd you get that?" asked Jodi.

"I made it out of strings and slime," said Harper. **"IT'S CALLED A LEAD,** and it will let us bring Michael G with us wherever we go. Even onto a boat."

"I just thought of something," said Theo.

"Maybe we should bring more than one of the mooshrooms with us. In case anything happens to this one along the way."

Jodi's jaw dropped. "Nothing's going to happen to Michael G. I promised him that!"

Theo frowned. "I'm not sure I'd have made that promise," he said. "We're debuffed, and we have a long way to walk. The cow could be attacked by any number of hostile mobs, or even struck with an arrow or a fireball meant for one of us."

Jodi put her hands to Michael G's head, as if blocking the mooshroom's ears. "Theo!" she protested. "He can hear you."

"All I'm trying to say is we might have trouble protecting him," Theo replied.

"In that case, we're better off with just one mooshroom," said Harper. **"SO WE CAN ALL**

FOCUS ON PROTECTING HIM. Right?"

Theo scratched his head. "Yeah, actually, that does make sense."

Jodi let out a sigh of relief. She sometimes forgot that arguing with Theo usually lead to a dead end. It was much easier to get him to see the logic behind their choices than to appeal to his emotions. Fortunately, Harper was there to act as a translator when they needed it.

Jodi took the lead from Harper. **She placed it around Michael G and used it to guide him onto her small boat.**

Seconds later, they were all speeding across the water back to the mainland.

It was night, and the low moon was nearly touching the calm water. Jodi smiled. In a weird way, she realized, she had gotten her wish. **For the moment, she had a pet.**

Everything was going really well . . .

. . . until the underwater zombie attacked.

It was called a drowned, and they never saw it coming. One second, everything was calm. The next, a trident burst from the water. It smashed into Morgan, knocking him off his boat.

"Morgan!" Jodi cried as her brother disappeared beneath the surface.

"I'LL HELP YOUR BROTHER," Po told her. "You stay here and protect Michael!"

Po dove beneath the waves, and Jodi thought: *That is one brave chicken.* She stayed close to Michael, holding his lead tight with one hand as she gripped her shield with the other.

Nearby, Harper and Theo equipped their bows, aiming arrows at the water. But all was still and quiet.

Suddenly there was a great splash of water beside Jodi's boat. She held up her shield just in time. **The drowned was right in front of her.** It had hopped into her boat and started pounding its fists against her shield.

Harper and Theo launched arrows at the enemy, but they hardly did any damage at all. Jodi wanted to flee, but she didn't dare leave the mooshroom to fend for itself.

Just then, the sun peeked above the horizon. Jodi could see her enemy more clearly in the early-morning light. She saw its tattered clothing. **She saw its eerie blue-green eyes.**

Then it burst into flame!

Jodi had momentarily forgotten that zombies—even underwater zombies—couldn't bear the light of the sun.

Between the fire and the arrows, the mob fell quickly. It croaked out a final moan; then it was gone.

Morgan and Po poked their heads out of the water.

"Is everyone okay?" Morgan asked. "The drowned gave us the slip."

Jodi realized she was still holding her breath. She exhaled and said, "We took care of it. With a little help from the sunlight." She looked at where the drowned had stood just a moment before. **"ALL THAT'S LEFT OF THAT ZOMBIE IS SOME ROTTEN FLESH AND A TRIDENT."**

"That's great news," Harper said from her boat. "Hold on to that trident. We'll need it later."

"If you say so," said Jodi, and she scooped up the weapon. "Can I leave the icky flesh behind?"

"Actually," said Harper, and she broke into a huge grin, "I think I've got a use for that, too." She looked around at her friends. **"ANYBODY UP FOR A LITTLE DETOUR?"**

Chapter 8

PUT YOUR PAWS TOGETHER FOR JODI'S ALL-PURPOSE PET SERVICE!

Back in the real world, it had been several days since Jodi had shown her presentation to her parents. Several days since they had told her "We'll see." And in that time, Jodi had begun to worry that Morgan was right. **Maybe she had gotten her hopes up too soon.**

That was when Jodi decided she needed to prove herself. She needed a *plan.*

She had started with their next-door neighbor. Miss Maribelle was a small woman with two large dogs. **Beefy, a muscular German shepherd,** liked to tug at his leash. **Bo, an energetic Labrador,** tried to chase

everything that moved. Miss Maribelle had to
walk them one at a time so they wouldn't drag her
all over town.

Jodi offered to walk Beefy and Bo in the
mornings, to give her neighbor a break.

At the dog park, Jodi had met other dog owners.

Some of them asked Jodi if she would walk their dogs from time to time. Some of them even offered to pay!

It was a dream come true. Getting paid *money* to spend time with animals? She said yes to everyone who asked.

Including one very familiar face.

"I can't believe you're going to walk Doc's dog," Po told her as they moved along the sidewalk. "In fact, I can't believe Doc is a dog person! **Are you sure she isn't paying you to walk a killer robot?**"

"I'm sure," Jodi said, and she tugged on Bo's leash to keep him on the sidewalk. "I met her dog at the park just the other day."

Po narrowed his eyes. "So it's a very *convincing* killer robot," he said. "With a fur suit and everything."

Jodi shrugged. **"Only if killer robots love to eat Vegan pepperoni,"** she said.

It was early in the morning, but there was no school for the entire week—and that meant no basketball practice for Po. He had offered to tag along, just so he had something to do.

The others were also coming along, simply out of curiosity. **They'd never seen a teacher's house before!**

"I bet Doc has a smart home," said Harper. "With all the latest gadgets."

"In that case, look out for stray lasers," said Theo. "Doc can be a real menace around technology, if you haven't noticed."

"**We've noticed,**" said Morgan. "Believe me, we've noticed." **Doc wasn't just responsible for their special VR goggles.** It had been her experiments with AI, or artificial intelligence, that had led to the unintended creation of the Evoker King.

But if they were expecting a high-tech wonderland, they were disappointed. From the outside, Doc's house looked just like any other— with the exception of a souped-up antenna on the roof. Harper grinned at the sight of the device. "**She probably gets channels from Alpha Centauri on that thing!**" she said happily.

As soon as Doc answered the door, a poodle

bounded out onto the porch. The dog shook its pom-pom tail at the sight of Jodi.

"Hello, Nicolaus Pupernicus!" Jodi cooed. "I'm happy to see you, too. Yes, I am!"

"Students! Greetings," Doc said brightly. "I hope you're enjoying your time off."

"We are now," said Po as he scratched the poodle behind its ears. "What a cutie!"

"He *is* cute," agreed Doc. "He's also crafty! He takes after his mama." Doc chuckled to herself. "He's even found a way to slip out of his collar once or twice. If he gets away from you, call him back with this, and he'll come running."

Doc handed Jodi a strange piece of high-tech equipment. It looked a little like a flute . . . mixed with a spaceship.

"What is it?" asked Jodi.

The teacher bounced on the tips of her toes. **"Why, it's a dog whistle of my own design!"** said Doc.

"I guess now we know what Doc does with her time off," Morgan whispered, and Harper quickly shushed him.

"I've heard about dog whistles," said Jodi. She turned to her friends. "Dogs have very sensitive ears. They can hear sounds that are too high-pitched for human ears. That's what a dog whistle does. It makes a sound that only dogs can hear." She turned back to Doc. **"But why is this one so, um . . . complicated?"**

"I've made great improvements to it," said Doc. "Think about it: Why make a *single* silent note when you can play an entire silent *symphony*? I think you'll agree that dogs deserve to enjoy music that is more sophisticated than a simple whistle can deliver." **Doc handed Jodi a thick instruction manual.** "It looks complicated, but it's really quite simple once you get the hang of it. Play 'Claire de Lune' to get him to sit, Beethoven's Fifth to get him to come to you, and

'Mary Had a Little Lamb' to get him to play dead."

"Got it," said Po. "I think."

As Jodi led the dogs away from Doc's porch, Po reached for the whistle. "This I've got to try," he said.

But Jodi pulled back, keeping the whistle out

of his grasp. **"Po, this isn't a toy!"** She shoved the instruction manual into his hands instead. "If you really want to use it, you'll have to make sure you're doing it right. Otherwise you could scare the poor things."

"Blargh," said Po. "Reading? On my day off? Forget it!"

"Wow," said Morgan. "Normally you go along with Po's mischief, Jodi."

"Well." Jodi lifted her chin defiantly. "I happen to take my responsibilities very seriously, if you didn't know."

Morgan surrendered. "Point taken."

"Can I at least give them treats?" asked Po.

"Yes, but you'll have to be careful. Nicolaus is lactose intolerant, and we have to wrap Beefy's vitamins in cheese. You do not *want* to get them mixed up. Oh! And Bo sometimes eats his treats

too fast, so you have to cut them up into little pieces first."

As Jodi dug through her bag of treats, she caught Morgan giving her a weird look. "What?" she asked him.

"It's nothing," he said. "It's just that I'm starting to think that maybe I was . . . I was . . ."

Morgan couldn't finish his sentence. He sneezed so loudly, it made the dogs howl.

"Gesundheit," said Po. "Hey, are you feeling all right?"

"Now that you mention it, I feel a little . . . debuffed at the moment." He chuckled at his own joke. "I hope I'm not getting sick while we're

on break. Wouldn't that be typical?"

"**No getting sick!**" said Harper. "We have to play Minecraft later."

"Yeah, Michael G is depending on us," said Po.

"That's not actually true," said Theo. "But I'm anxious to get back to our quest, too."

"Count on it," said Morgan, and he sniffled. "**Nothing's going to stop us from getting that cure.**"

Chapter 9

ONE MOB'S ROTTEN FLESH IS ANOTHER MOB'S TREASURE. (BUT SERIOUSLY, I'D RATHER HAVE THE EMERALDS!)

Theo recognized the Minecraft village immediately.

"We've been here before," he said. **"THESE ARE THE VILLAGERS WE SAVED FROM THE GIANT CAVE SPIDER."**

"That's right," said Harper. "And one of them is a cleric, remember? Help me find that one."

Now Theo was *really* curious. "What do you need a cleric for?" he asked.

"It's a surprise," Harper said. Her avatar smiled. **"TRUST ME. I'VE GOT A PLAN!"**

That was good enough for Theo. He *did* trust Harper, and her plans tended to be good ones, so he set out in search of a cleric.

As Theo looked around the village, he saw that the square Minecraft sun was low in the sky. That made him anxious. **Theo had grown to fear the night,** because that was when it was hardest to avoid hostile mobs.

Working together, the kids were still more than a match for any danger in Minecraft. Theo knew that. But they were running low on supplies. They were eating through their apples and bread too quickly. And they had used almost all of their arrows.

They were nearly back to the swamp, though. **Once they got there, they could trade the mooshroom for a cure.** And this whole nightmare would be behind them.

As Theo stepped onto a cobblestone pathway, he felt something nudge him from behind. He turned to see Michael G close behind him.

"AW, HE LIKES YOU!" said Jodi. "I dropped his lead to let him graze for a while, and he went right to you."

Theo sighed. "He doesn't *like* me," he argued.

"He doesn't like *anything.* He's incapable of it. **HE'S JUST COMPUTER CODE WEARING A COW SUIT.**"

Jodi harumphed. "Well, he's not going to like you for much longer if you keep saying things like that!"

Just then, the sun dipped below the horizon. Theo felt his anxiety grow. "Keep a grip on Bessie's lead, okay?" he said. **"THE TOWN'S TORCHES SHOULD KEEP ANY HOSTILE MOBS FROM SPAWNING, BUT MONSTERS COULD ALWAYS CREEP IN FROM OUTSIDE."**

"Don't listen to him, Michael," Jodi said, taking the lead. "He knows your name. He's just being silly."

Theo watched the villagers as they started returning to their homes for the night. **He saw that Harper had found the cleric,** and he walked over to see if she needed any help.

"I traded a stack of rotten flesh for emeralds," she told him. "And now I'll use the emeralds to buy some lapis."

"Lapis?" Theo echoed. "You must be enchanting something."

"You guessed it. Check it out!" Harper held up her brand-new piece of lapis lazuli. It shone bright blue in the torchlight. **"HEY, JODI, CAN I HAVE THAT TRIDENT?"**

With the trident and the lapis in her inventory, Harper dropped an enchantment table right in the middle of town. Next, she placed a series of bookshelves around it.

"I love libraries, too," Jodi said. "But are you sure you want to build one in the middle of a sidewalk?"

"THE BOOKSHELVES WILL MAKE MY ENCHANTMENT MORE POWERFUL," Harper said. "And get me the enchantment I want."

"What enchantment do you want?" Jodi asked.

"I've been trying to guess," Theo said. "But I'm stumped."

"Channeling," Harper answered. "We'll still need to wait for a thunderstorm," she explained further. "But with a trident that's enchanted with Channeling, we won't have to rely on luck for lightning to strike. **WE'LL BE ABLE TO CALL DOWN A BOLT OF ELECTRICITY FROM A THUNDERCLOUD.**"

Theo wished he had fingers that he could snap. He settled for a little hop. "And the lightning will change Michael G from red to brown. Brilliant!"

"I just hope this works," said Harper. She bent over the enchanting table. "I might not get Channeling **ON MY FIRST TRY.** You should get a grindstone ready, in case we need to start over."

But she was worried for no reason. Theo could tell by the way she smiled. **The enchanting had worked perfectly.**

Harper whooped in triumph, and she held up the enchanted trident for all to see. It glittered purple in the night. The kids fell silent as they looked at it in awe.

And in the momentary silence . . . **Theo heard a hiss.**

Theo whirled around in alarm. His fears were true. He saw the creeper sneaking up behind Jodi and Michael. He saw it . . .

Too late.

With a sudden burst of light and sound, the creeper exploded. Jodi and the mooshroom both flashed red as **they were knocked forward by the force of the blast.**

Theo held his breath. Would the mooshroom survive? It couldn't possibly have much health, could it? If only there were something he could do!

That's when Theo remembered: he had one precious **splash Potion of Healing** in his inventory. He'd been saving it for an emergency.

He figured this fit the bill.

Acting quickly, he hurled the potion at the mooshroom. The flask shattered, and the life-restoring liquid washed over the animal.

"Ow," said Jodi, rubbing her head. "What hit us?"

"IT WAS A CREEPER," said Harper. "It came out of nowhere! Are you okay?"

"And is Michael G okay?" asked Theo.

A smile broke across Jodi's square face. "Aw, you care about him."

Theo cleared his throat. "No, I don't. I just don't want to have to go all the way back to that island to find another one."

"Sure, that's it," said Jodi, but she didn't sound convinced. "Did you hear, Michael G? He even got your name right!"

Harper and Jodi laughed as Morgan and Po hurried over to check on them. **They all doted on the mooshroom, who mooed with**

pleasure at the attention.

When Michael G turned its big, bovine eyes to Theo, he couldn't help himself.

He gave the mooshroom a little pat on the head.

For a string of computer code . . . this cow was pretty cute.

Chapter 10

SMALL BUSINESS OWNERSHIP! IT'S LIKE PUTTING THE WHOLE WORLD ON A LEASH AND HAVING IT DRAG YOU AROUND.

In the real world, Morgan was feeling sicker with each passing day. He was almost paranoid enough to believe it had something to do with the witch's curse. But if that was true, shouldn't his friends be sick, too?

Jodi, for one, seemed healthier than ever. **As her pet-walking service got more popular, she seemed to have more and more energy.**

The one thing she seemed unable to do . . . was to say no.

"I thought you were a *dog*

walker," said Po. "What's that guy doing here?" And he pointed at an iguana on a leash.

"The iguana makes more sense than the fish," said Theo, **and he tapped at the goldfish bowl in Po's lap.**

"You leave Bubbles out of this!" said Po. "She just wanted some fresh air."

Theo rolled his eyes. "I think fresh air is the *last* thing a water-breather wants."

"Are you sure we can't take some of those leashes for you?" asked Harper.

Jodi shot her brother a quick look before answering. "No, no," she said. "I'm fine. I'm good! **Super responsible, that's me.**"

Morgan could only sneeze in reply.

Jodi was holding leashes for no fewer than six dogs, one iguana, and a birdcage on wheels. Somehow, she managed to keep all the animals on the path. Even Baron Sweetcheeks, in his plastic exercise ball, was careful to stay close to her. Morgan and Jodi had volunteered to care for the hamster during the school break, and **Jodi hadn't wanted to leave him home alone.**

Suddenly, the hamster squeaked as if excited. **He rolled ahead of the group.** It seemed like he recognized a woman on the path ahead of them. She was pushing a baby stroller and wearing large sunglasses.

When she took off her sunglasses and smiled at them, Morgan recognized her, too. **It was Ms. Minerva, their homeroom teacher.**

"Baron Sweetcheeks, is that you?" she said. "And my favorite students are all here! I almost couldn't see you past all those . . . dogs."

The way she said the word, Morgan figured something out right away: Ms. Minerva was *not* a dog person.

"Hi, Ms. Minerva!" said Harper. "I didn't know you had a baby."

Ms. Minerva laughed. "Just my fur baby. This is Dewey." She pulled the cover of the stroller back, revealing an orange-striped cat, crooked whiskers, and a very annoyed expression. **"He's an indoor cat,"** she said by way of explanation.

Morgan had never seen a cat in a baby stroller before. But he had learned a long time ago that adults did some very strange things.

Suddenly, Jodi lurched forward. One of the dogs had taken an interest in Ms. Minerva's cat, and now he tugged against his leash.

"Wait, is that . . . is that Doc's dog?" asked Ms. Minerva, suddenly alarmed. **"Oh, no. There's bad blood between these two. . . ."**

Time seemed to freeze. Morgan held his breath as dog and cat locked eyes. He saw Jodi's grip

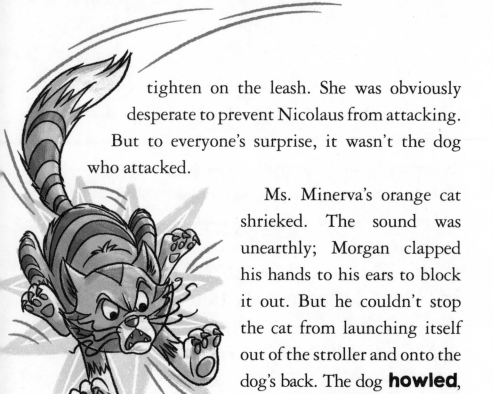

tighten on the leash. She was obviously desperate to prevent Nicolaus from attacking. But to everyone's surprise, it wasn't the dog who attacked.

Ms. Minerva's orange cat shrieked. The sound was unearthly; Morgan clapped his hands to his ears to block it out. But he couldn't stop the cat from launching itself out of the stroller and onto the dog's back. The dog **howled**, the cat **hissed**, and **Jodi cried out in surprise.**

The animals all panicked, pulling in eight different directions at once.

Jodi fell. She lost her grip on the leashes. **And the pets went wild.**

Chapter 11

WHO LET THE DOGS OUT? AND COULD THAT PERSON PLEASE COME GET THEM?

Jodi couldn't believe this was happening.

All she'd wanted was to show her brother that she could be responsible. That she could take care of animals. Every sort of animal!

And now those animals were scattered all over a public park. They were people's beloved pets . . . and they were lost. All lost.

All her fault.

"Dewey!" cried Ms. Minerva, and she ran off after the cat. "Dewey Decimal, come back here!"

Jodi fought back tears. "I lost them. I can't believe I lost them."

"Uh, well, not *all* of them," Po said. He held up the fishbowl. "Bubbles here stuck around."

Jodi couldn't fight the tears anymore. She stood there in the middle of the park, her knees skinned and her fingers sore, and she cried.

Then she felt her brother's arms around her. **He gave her a good long hug**—then he gripped her by her shoulders and he looked her in the eyes.

"We can fix this, Jodi," he said. "But we can't do it without you."

"M-me?" Jodi said.

"You know these animals," he said. "You know them extremely well. And you can tell us what we need to do to get them back." He smiled. "You just have to believe in yourself. Like I believe in you."

Jodi almost wanted to cry again, hearing that. But there was no more time for tears.

Those animals needed her.

"Okay," she said, wiping her cheeks. "Here's what we're going to do. Polly always wants a cracker. Theo, get the parrot back by giving her as many treats as it takes. Harper, same idea for the iguana—but give him fruit, not crackers." Theo and Harper grabbed the treats from Jodi, saluted, and ran off.

She rubbed her chin. "We could round up the dogs if we knew how to use Doc's whistle. . . ."

"Oh!" said Po. "I know how to use it. **I read the instruction manual last night!"**

Morgan gave him a suspicious look. "Really?"

"Why is that so hard to believe?" Po asked. "I'm a reluctant reader, sure. But Doc is an absolute

poet." He turned to Jodi. "I can do it. I know I can. Beethoven's Fifth Symphony, right? Consider it done-done-done-*donnne.*"

"**I trust you, Po,**" said Jodi. "And Pupernicus is a natural-born leader. If he comes running, the others will follow." She paused. "That just leaves Ms. Minerva's cat."

"So what do cats like?" asked Morgan. He thought about it for a moment, and his eyes went to the goldfish.

Po covered Bubbles with his body. **"Don't even think about it!"** he cried.

Jodi snapped her fingers. "I've got it!" She dug around in her bag until she found the laser pointer she'd used for her presentation. "Cats love to chase laser pointers. We'll get him back in no time."

Morgan grinned. "I knew you'd think of something."

"Thinking is only half the battle," said Jodi. "Go, go, go!"

It took nearly an hour. Po blew the whistle until he was out of breath—and surrounded by a captive canine audience. Theo had to climb a tree to reach the parrot. And to her embarrassment, **Harper captured the wrong lizard on her first attempt.** She had to go back and find the right one all over again.

But as Jodi used the laser pointer to lure Dewey back into Ms. Minerva's waiting stroller, they all breathed big sighs of relief.

"Ms. Minerva, I am so sorry," Jodi said. "I take full responsibility for that."

"Nonsense," said Ms. Minerva. She was wiping grass stains from her clothes. **"I should have**

recognized that
dog of Doc's in time to keep
things from getting out of hand.

Or maybe I should put a seat belt in this thing."
She patted the stroller. "But in the end, no harm
was done."

For a moment, Jodi believed that. She thought
everything was fine.

But then she saw shattered plastic in the grass.
She recognized it right away. Somehow, in all the
commotion, Baron Sweetcheeks's ball had broken
into pieces.

The hamster was lying unconscious
atop the wreckage.

"Baron Sweetcheeks!"
cried Jodi. "He's hurt!"

Chapter 12

SWEET OF CHEEKS.
STRONG OF SPIRIT.
INJURED OF PAW.

Jodi was so nervous in the waiting room of the vet, she thought she would shake apart into a million tiny bits.

Morgan held her hand, and **Ms. Minerva promised that everything would be okay.** But Jodi felt sick to know that Baron Sweetcheeks had been injured. And it had happened when she was supposed to be taking care of him!

"Your hamster will be fine," promised the veterinarian. She was a young woman with a kind voice. "It's only a sprained paw."

"I didn't know hamsters could get sprains," said Ms. Minerva.

"It's actually very common," said the vet. **"I love hamsters, but they tend to get underfoot."**

"What's the treatment?" Morgan asked.

"He just needs rest," said the vet. "The injury will heal on its own. In a few weeks, he'll be as good as new."

A few weeks? Jodi wanted to sink into her seat. **It was good news, mostly.** But she felt bad

that he would need so long to recover.

"**I gave him a little medicine to calm him down,**" said the vet. "So he's sleeping now, if you'd like to see him?"

The veterinarian led Jodi and Morgan into the back room, where Baron Sweetcheeks lay sleeping on a pillow. His adorable, super-pinchable cheeks puffed in and out with each little breath.

"It's all my fault," Jodi said. "You were right all along, Morgan. **I . . . I'm not ready for a pet of my own.**"

Morgan shook his head. His nose twitched. "That's not what I—I—"

He covered his nose and mouth just before letting out a tremendous sneeze.

"Bless you!" said the vet.

"Thanks," said Morgan. "I think I'm getting a cold."

"Think again," said the vet. "I can see exactly what's going on. **You're highly allergic.**"

"Allergic?" echoed Morgan.

The vet nodded. "To dogs and cats, yes." She smiled. "I'm assuming you don't have any at home."

Jodi swallowed hard. "No, we don't," she said. She looked at her brother as he wiped his nose. "And now . . . we never will."

Chapter 13

THEY SAY LIGHTNING NEVER STRIKES TWICE. BUT "THEY" DON'T HAVE A TRIDENT OF CHANNELING.

When they returned to Minecraft, Po and the others had just a short way to go until they would arrive at the witch's hut. And the brown mooshroom she was expecting . . . **was still red.**

Po had other things on his mind, though.

"YOU GUYS . . . I THINK I WANT A GOLDFISH," he said.

Morgan glared at him. **"NOT NOW, PO."**

"But—"

Morgan cleared his throat and inclined his head in Jodi's direction. She had been quiet ever since the incident in the park. Obviously, her own plan to get a pet was not going well.

"Sorry," said Po, realizing that he hadn't been thinking of Jodi's feelings. He moved to her side and pushed his blocky shoulder against hers. "Hey, cheer up, kid," he said. **"I'M SURE YOU'LL GET A PET EVENTUALLY."**

Jodi frowned. "Baron Sweetcheeks is limping. And my brother sneezes every time he even looks at a dog." She shook her head sadly. "I think this is one dream I have to let go."

"Well, Morgan's older than you, so he has to move out one day, right?" Po snickered, but Jodi didn't respond to his joke.

"Seriously, though," said Po. "What happened to the Baron wasn't your fault." As soon as Po said that word, he realized something. **"HEY. THE FAULT,"** he said. **"I CAN'T SEE IT."**

"It's the storm clouds," said Jodi. "They sort of suit my mood today."

Rain had already begun to fall. "Yeah, normally I hate stormy weather," Po said. "But today, it's just what we need."

"This is perfect!" said Harper. **"IT'S TIME TO CALL DOWN SOME LIGHTNING.** Jodi, you

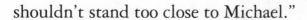

shouldn't stand too close to Michael."

"Can I do it, Harper?" asked Po. **"CAN I THROW THE TRIDENT?"**

Harper didn't seem too sure about that. "You know how important this is, right?"

"Yes!" said Po. "I can be serious. You've seen me play basketball, right?" He crossed his chicken-wing arms. "I've got great aim, and I don't choke under pressure."

Harper handed over the trident. **It still glowed with magic.** "Just don't throw it directly at the mooshroom," said Harper. "A block or two away from him will work fine."

"Got it," said Po. "More like a lightning rod, less like a steak fork."

As the rain fell harder, Po gripped the trident tight.

He lined up the shot.

He threw it . . .

. . . and he missed his target by several yards.

"What was that?!" asked Morgan.

"Sorry!" said Po. "I was distracted by that pig."

They all turned to look. Po was right—a pig

had wandered up to them. It saw the trident stuck in the ground nearby, and, curious, it approached the enchanted weapon and gave it a sniff.

Just then, **a great bolt of lightning shot down** from the heavens.

Po turned away from the searing brightness.

And when he turned back . . . the pig had

been transformed. Standing where the cute little animal had been, there was now a strange creature that appeared half pig and half human . . . with its face partially melted away to reveal a gleaming skull.

"**PIGLIN!**" he cried. He pulled his sword from his inventory. "It's a zombified piglin!"

"I thought they only spawned in the Nether," said Jodi. She hurried back to Michael's side, raising her shield.

"Let's everybody stay calm," whispered Morgan. "They aren't hostile, remember? **IF WE DON'T ATTACK IT, THEN IT WON'T ATTACK US.**"

Po found that hard to believe. The mob looked dangerous. **It was even holding a sword**

made of solid gold! But the zombified piglin sniffed again at the trident, looked around at the kids, and shuffled off into the storm.

Po had a funny feeling they hadn't seen the last of it.

"Let's try this again," said Jodi. She led the mooshroom over to the trident, gave him a quick kiss on the nose for luck, and then dropped the lead and ran clear.

It was only a few seconds before lightning struck again.

This time, it found its target. Michael G stood transformed . . . a brown mooshroom at last.

"**MOO?**" he said, and he looked at them with big questioning eyes.

"Look at that face!" said Theo, and he giggled. Everybody else joined in.

Chapter 14

WHICH WITCH ORDERED THE MOOSHROOM?

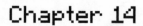

The witch cackled from the door of the hut, utterly gleeful at the sight of Michael G. The mob came down from the porch, skipping happily to a specially prepared cage. **The cage had a floor of mycelium, and tiny mushrooms grew around its edges.** For a moment, Jodi thought that perhaps Michael would be happy here.

She hesitated, though, when the witch opened the gate to the cage. The witch reached impatiently for Michael's leash, and Jodi knew she didn't have a choice. "Sorry, buddy," she said to the cow. **Then she handed the lead to the witch,** who

locked the mooshroom in his new cage.

"HIS NAME IS MICHAEL G," said Theo. "He likes wheat and gentle pats on the head. You'd better treat him right."

"Treat, hrm," said the witch. "Trick, hah."

And then the witch drew a gleaming **netherite sword**.

Jodi took a step back. "What is that for?" she asked.

"A powerful spell, heh, will I cast," said the witch. "Many, hrm, *ingredients,* has it. Chicken feather. Wool of,

hah, sheep. Horn of, hrm, goat." **The witch grinned maliciously.** "And leather . . . from a brown mooshroom . . . SLAIN BY SWORD."

"Slain?!" said Jodi.

"The witch is going to destroy Michael G for his leather!" said Morgan.

"No," said Theo. **"THAT IS NOT GOING TO HAPPEN."** And he readied his sword.

The witch still smiled. "Weak, you are."

"You're right," said Harper. "We're still weakened."

"That's why we phoned a friend," said Po.

The kids stepped aside . . . **and Ash leaped forward, swinging her sword.**

It was a direct hit. The witch fell back, screeching and flashing red. Ash—who hadn't been debuffed like the others—had clearly done a lot of damage with that attack.

"Are you sure about this, everybody?" Ash asked. "If we defeat the witch . . . you might never be cured."

"We're sure," said Jodi.

"WE CAN'T LET THE WITCH HURT THAT MOOSHROOM," said Theo. "It just . . . it isn't right."

"In that case, everybody, start opening cages!" said Ash. She gripped her sword. "I'll keep the witch busy."

"Hah!" said the witch, throwing a splash potion at the group.

"Scatter!" said Morgan, and they all dove in different directions.

Theo was too slow.

The potion hit him square in the back. **"YEOW!"** he said.

"LEAVE THEM ALONE!" cried Ash, and she took another swing.

Jodi hurried to Theo's side. "Are you all right?" she asked him.

"I'm fine," Theo insisted. "Get Michael out of here!"

Jodi waited for her moment to act. She watched as Ash swung her sword again, and the witch melted into the shadows. Then Jodi sprang into action, running to Michael's cage and throwing open the door.

"GET OUT OF HERE, BUDDY!" she cried.

As a parrot flew overhead and a fox rushed past her, Jodi realized her friends were hard at work all the way down the line of cages. She saw her brother hurrying toward the baby panda's cell.

But then the witch slipped from the shadows just beside him.

"Morgan!" Jodi cried in warning, but it was too late. **The witch hurled a potion.** By the time it had shattered against him, the mob was already gone again.

"I can't keep up!" said Ash, running past Jodi and swinging her sword at every shadow. "How is that witch moving so quickly?"

Strangely, the witch showed little interest in Ash. The mob stayed clear of Ash's sword. Instead of fighting back, **the witch hurled potion after potion over Ash's head.**

Theo and Morgan had already been hit.

Harper was next.

And then Jodi was struck.

But to her surprise . . . it didn't hurt.

In fact . . . it felt good.

"What was in that splash potion?" Jodi asked.

Theo and Harper exchanged a look. **"I FEEL STRONGER,"** said Harper.

"The witch buffed us back to our normal stats," said Theo.

"I don't know what that means!" said Ash as she swung her sword.

"Ash, stop!" said Morgan. "It means . . . it means the witch cured us!"

Ash was just about to bring her sword down on

the witch. She stopped her swing just in time.

The witch cackled. This time, instead of sounding menacing, the laughter had a friendly tone to it.

"I don't understand," said Ash, poised for action. She didn't dare take her eyes off the mob. "What's going on here?"

"A, HRM, TEST," said the witch. "To see . . . see if you care. If beings of flesh and blood . . . can care about *them*." The witch waved an arm at the animal mobs around them.

Ash put down her sword. "Of course we care."

Jodi nodded. "All of us do," she agreed. "Right, guys?"

Theo stepped forward. He put a hand on Jodi's shoulder. "That's right."

The witch nodded, cackling again, but more quietly. "Hrm . . . be good to them. Be good, heh, to each other." With bright green eyes, the witch looked at them all, one at a time. "Your compassion, hah. You will need it. Need it, hrm, for what comes next." Those green eyes sparkled. **"SAVE THE BEES."**

"Save the bees?" Harper echoed. "What does that mean?"

The witch didn't answer. The strange mob just lifted an arm and waved at the animals, as if telling them good-bye. Slowly, that arm began to glow . . . and then it shattered, transforming into a swirling mass of butterflies. They swept over Ash, swirled around Jodi, **and then soared into the sky.**

And there, in the murky swamp water where the witch had stood, was the right arm of the Evoker King.

"I PROMISE. We do care about them," Jodi said to the night sky. "We care about this whole world. Even if it *is* digital . . . it's real to us."

"Hear, hear," Theo agreed.

The clouds parted, and **Jodi felt her heart surge with new hope.**

But then she saw the Fault. It was even larger than before.

And she couldn't help wondering if this digital world they loved . . . might be in terrible danger.

Chapter 15

WITH GREAT HAMSTERS THERE MUST COME . . . GREAT RESPONSIBILITY!

Jodi spent the rest of the week nursing Baron Sweetcheeks back to health. She also continued to walk her neighbors' dogs . . . but she had learned not to walk them all at once. **Taking one or two at a time took her longer, but she was happy to spend her vacation in the company of so many animals.**

She had surprised her parents when she'd told them that she had changed her mind about having a pet. She wasn't certain that she was ready yet for that much responsibility. And even if she was, she couldn't stand to see Morgan suffer. His allergies were pretty severe (and he didn't always cover his mouth when he sneezed, either).

But Jodi had no idea what awaited her when she returned to Stonesword Library the following weekend. All her friends had gathered in the meeting room, along with Mr. Malory, Ms. Minerva, and Doc. **Even Baron Sweetcheeks was there,** and Ash had once again dialed in on Theo's laptop.

And best of all, right on top of the meeting room's central table, there was a large gift with a big bow on it.

"It was your brother's idea," Mr. Malory explained. "And your teachers convinced me that you're ready for it." He slid the box across the table. **"Go ahead and open it."**

Jodi tore away the gift wrap, and she was stunned by what she saw.

It was a brand-new hamster cage . . . with a brand-new hamster inside.

"It only seems fair," said Mr. Malory.

"Woodsword has a class hamster. Shouldn't Stonesword have one as well?"

"We thought you could care for her, Jodi," said Doc. "So that you can get practice caring for a pet, with help from your friends and under adult supervision."

"She'll stay here at the library," Ms. Minerva explained. **"But she'll be your responsibility. You even get to name her."**

Jodi's eyes filled with tears. **The hamster's cheeks . . . her cute little tail . . . it was like a dream come true.**

"I promise I'll take care of you," Jodi told the hamster.

Morgan put a hand on her shoulder. "I know you'll do a great job," he said. "And one day, when you're ready for a puppy or a kitten of your own . . . I promise I'll get an allergy shot."

Jodi gasped. **"But you're so afraid of needles!"**

"Well, yeah, I am," said Morgan, blushing. "But I won't let that stand in the way of your happiness."

Jodi gave him a big hug. Then she went around the room and gave everyone else a hug, fist bump, or high five. She "booped" Ash's nose on the laptop screen and patted Baron Sweetcheeks on his fuzzy head.

Then she cuddled Stonesword Library's new addition and said, "Welcome to the family, **Duchess Dimples.** I love you already!"

Everyone crowded around to give Duchess Dimples a proper welcome. It was a joyful moment that Jodi would remember forever.

But she saw a hint of worry in Harper's eyes. She noticed that Morgan was scratching his ear, like he sometimes did when he was nervous.

Save the bees. That's what the witch had said. And whatever that meant, they would have to figure it out soon.

They still had three more pieces of the Evoker King to find. Jodi knew in her heart that helping their digital friend—that putting him back together again—was one responsibility they couldn't put off any longer.

And to do that, they were going to have to go deeper into Minecraft than ever before. . . .

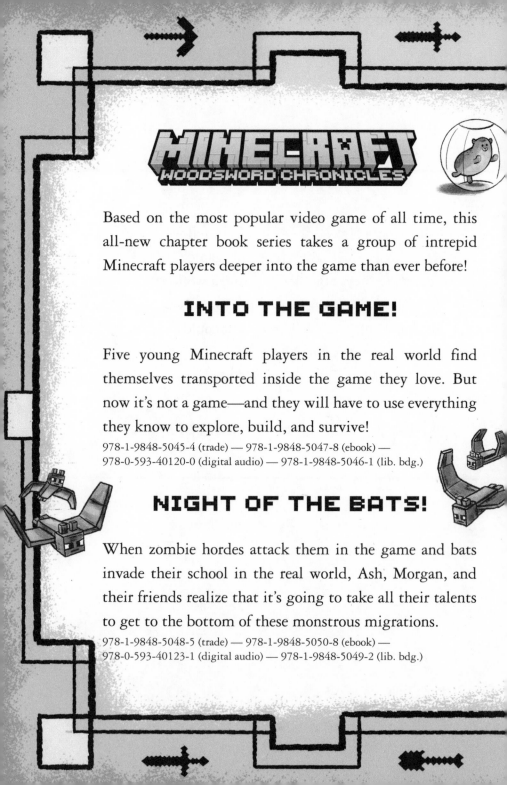

MINECRAFT
WOODSWORD CHRONICLES

Based on the most popular video game of all time, this all-new chapter book series takes a group of intrepid Minecraft players deeper into the game than ever before!

INTO THE GAME!

Five young Minecraft players in the real world find themselves transported inside the game they love. But now it's not a game—and they will have to use everything they know to explore, build, and survive!

978-1-9848-5045-4 (trade) — 978-1-9848-5047-8 (ebook) — 978-0-593-40120-0 (digital audio) — 978-1-9848-5046-1 (lib. bdg.)

NIGHT OF THE BATS!

When zombie hordes attack them in the game and bats invade their school in the real world, Ash, Morgan, and their friends realize that it's going to take all their talents to get to the bottom of these monstrous migrations.

978-1-9848-5048-5 (trade) — 978-1-9848-5050-8 (ebook) — 978-0-593-40123-1 (digital audio) — 978-1-9848-5049-2 (lib. bdg.)

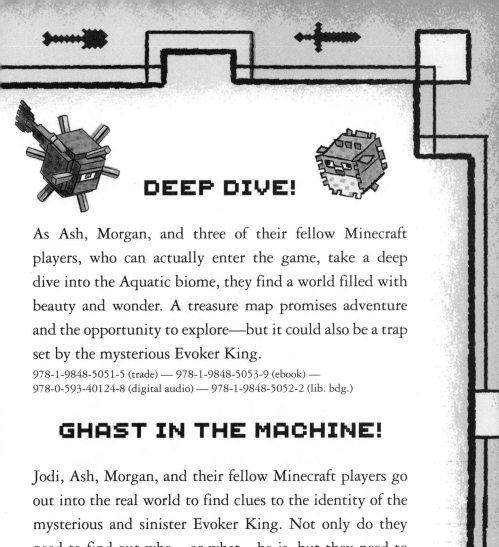

DEEP DIVE!

As Ash, Morgan, and three of their fellow Minecraft players, who can actually enter the game, take a deep dive into the Aquatic biome, they find a world filled with beauty and wonder. A treasure map promises adventure and the opportunity to explore—but it could also be a trap set by the mysterious Evoker King.

978-1-9848-5051-5 (trade) — 978-1-9848-5053-9 (ebook) — 978-0-593-40124-8 (digital audio) — 978-1-9848-5052-2 (lib. bdg.)

GHAST IN THE MACHINE!

Jodi, Ash, Morgan, and their fellow Minecraft players go out into the real world to find clues to the identity of the mysterious and sinister Evoker King. Not only do they need to find out who—or what—he is, but they need to know if it's really possible for him to escape the game!

978-1-9848-5062-1 (trade) — 978-1-9848-5064-5 (ebook) — 978-0-593-40126-2 (digital audio) — 978-1-9848-5063-8 (lib. bdg.)

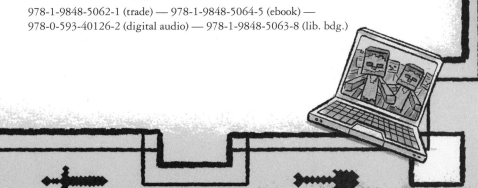

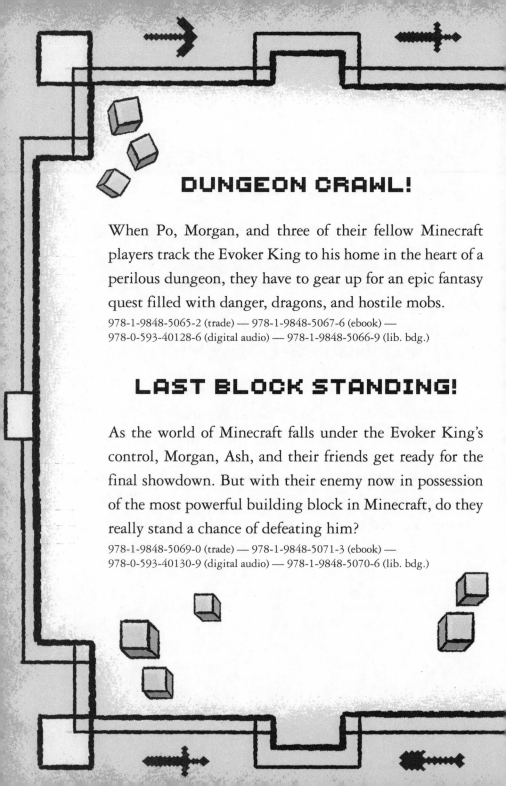

DUNGEON CRAWL!

When Po, Morgan, and three of their fellow Minecraft players track the Evoker King to his home in the heart of a perilous dungeon, they have to gear up for an epic fantasy quest filled with danger, dragons, and hostile mobs.

978-1-9848-5065-2 (trade) — 978-1-9848-5067-6 (ebook) — 978-0-593-40128-6 (digital audio) — 978-1-9848-5066-9 (lib. bdg.)

LAST BLOCK STANDING!

As the world of Minecraft falls under the Evoker King's control, Morgan, Ash, and their friends get ready for the final showdown. But with their enemy now in possession of the most powerful building block in Minecraft, do they really stand a chance of defeating him?

978-1-9848-5069-0 (trade) — 978-1-9848-5071-3 (ebook) — 978-0-593-40130-9 (digital audio) — 978-1-9848-5070-6 (lib. bdg.)

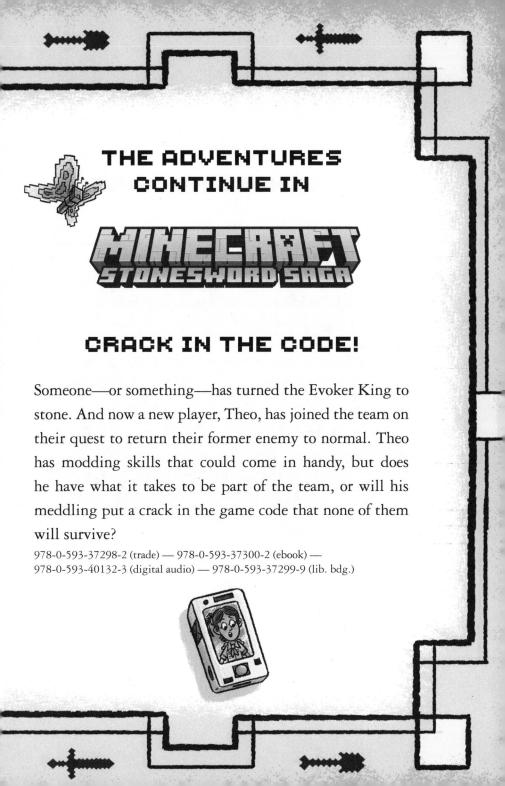

THE ADVENTURES CONTINUE IN

MINECRAFT
STONESWORD SAGA

CRACK IN THE CODE!

Someone—or something—has turned the Evoker King to stone. And now a new player, Theo, has joined the team on their quest to return their former enemy to normal. Theo has modding skills that could come in handy, but does he have what it takes to be part of the team, or will his meddling put a crack in the game code that none of them will survive?

978-0-593-37298-2 (trade) — 978-0-593-37300-2 (ebook) —
978-0-593-40132-3 (digital audio) — 978-0-593-37299-9 (lib. bdg.)

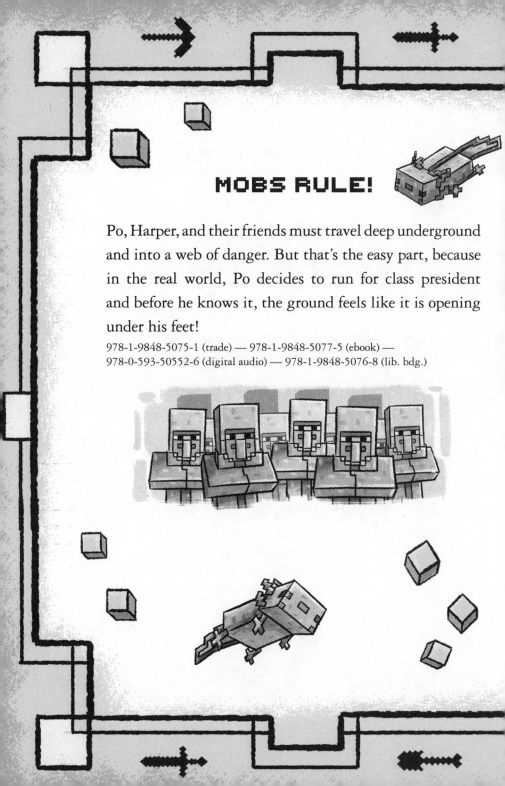

MOBS RULE!

Po, Harper, and their friends must travel deep underground and into a web of danger. But that's the easy part, because in the real world, Po decides to run for class president and before he knows it, the ground feels like it is opening under his feet!

978-1-9848-5075-1 (trade) — 978-1-9848-5077-5 (ebook) — 978-0-593-50552-6 (digital audio) — 978-1-9848-5076-8 (lib. bdg.)

MORE MINECRAFT
ADVENTURES
COMING SOON . . . !

MINECRAFT is a game about placing blocks and going on adventures. Build, play, and explore across infinitely generated worlds of mountains, caverns, oceans, jungles, and deserts. Defeat hordes of zombies, bake the cake of your dreams, venture to new dimensions, or build a skyscraper. What you do in Minecraft is up to you.

Nick Eliopulos is a writer who lives in Brooklyn (as many writers do). He likes to spend half his free time reading and the other half gaming. He cowrote the Adventurers Guild series with his best friend and works as a narrative designer for a small video game studio. After all these years, endermen still give him the creeps.

Alan Batson is a British cartoonist and illustrator. His works include *Everything I Need to Know I Learned from a Star Wars Little Golden Book, Everything That Glitters Is Guy!,* and *Spider-Ham.* Being extremely fond of cubes and travel to exotic places, he has recently begun to lend his talents to several different books on adventures in the world of Minecraft.

Chris Hill is an illustrator living in Birmingham, England, with his wife and two daughters and has been loving it for twenty-five years! When he's not working, he spends time with his family and trying to tire out his dog on long walks. If there's any time left after that, he loves to go riding on his motorcycle, feeling the wind on his face while contemplating his next illustration adventure.

JOURNEY INTO THE WORLD OF

—BOOKS FOR EVERY READING LEVEL—

OFFICIAL NOVELS:

FOR YOUNGER READERS:

OFFICIAL GUIDES:

DISCOVER MORE AT READMINECRAFT.COM

Penguin
Random
House